6/11 1x

4110

CR

WITHDRAWN

# SLIM GOODBODY'S NUTRITION EDITION

# Marvelous Meats and More

CRABTREE
Publishing Company
www.crabtreebooks.com

# Crabtree Publishing Company
## www.crabtreebooks.com

**Series development, writing, and packaging**:
John Burstein, Slim Goodbody Corp.

**Editors**:
Molly Aloian
Reagan Miller
Mark Sachner, Water Buffalo Books

**Editorial director**:
Kathy Middleton

**Production coordinator**:
Kenneth Wright

**Prepress technician:**
Kenneth Wright

**Designer**:
Tammy West, Westgraphix LLC

**Photos**:
Chris Pinchback, Pinchback Photography

**Photo credits:**
© Slim Goodbody, iStockphotos, and Shutterstock images.

"Slim Goodbody" and Pinchback photos, copyright,
© Slim Goodbody

**Acknowledgements**:
The author would like to thank the following people for their help in this project:
Christine Burstein, Olivia Davis, Kylie Fong, Nathan Levig, Havana Lyman, Andrew McBride, Lulu McClure, Ben McGinnis, Esme Power, Joe Ryan

"Slim Goodbody" and "Slim Goodbody's Nutrition Edition" are registered trademarks of the Slim Goodbody Corp.

**Library and Archives Canada Cataloguing in Publication**

Burstein, John
      Marvelous meats and more / John Burstein.

(Slim Goodbody's nutrition edition)
Includes index.
ISBN 978-0-7787-5044-4 (bound).--ISBN 978-0-7787-5059-8 (pbk.)

      1. Meat--Juvenile literature.  2. Proteins in human nutrition--Juvenile literature.  3. Nutrition--Juvenile literature.  I. Title.  II. Series:°Burstein, John.  Slim Goodbody's nutrition edition.

QP144.M43B87 2010          j641.3'6          C2009-903856-0

**Library of Congress Cataloging-in-Publication Data**

Burstein, John.
   Marvelous meats and more / John Burstein.
       p. cm. -- (Slim Goodbody's nutrition edition)
   Includes index.
   ISBN 978-0-7787-5044-4 (reinforced lib. bdg. : alk. paper) -- ISBN 978-0-7787-5059-8 (pbk. : alk. paper)
   1. Meats--Juvenile literature. 2. Nutrition--Juvenile literature. 3. Children--Nutrition--Requirements--Juvenile literature.  I. Title. II. Series.

   QP144.M43B87 2010
   613.2--dc22

                                      2009024571

# Crabtree Publishing Company
www.crabtreebooks.com          1-800-387-7650

**Published in Canada**
**Crabtree Publishing**
616 Welland Ave.
St. Catharines, Ontario
L2M 5V6

**Published in the United States**
**Crabtree Publishing**
PMB16A
350 Fifth Ave., Suite 3308
New York, NY  10118

**Published in the United Kingdom**
**Crabtree Publishing**
White Cross Mills
High Town, Lancaster
LA1 4XS

**Published in Australia**
**Crabtree Publishing**
386 Mt. Alexander Rd.
Ascot Vale (Melbourne)
VIC 3032

# CONTENTS

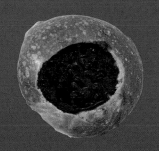

# GREETINGS

My name is Slim Goodbody.
I want to ask you two questions.

**1.** Do you like to eat good foods?
I hope you said **YES**.
**2.** What can help show you
what foods to eat?
I hope you said **THE**
**FOOD PYRAMID**.

The food pyramid helps you eat right.

4

There are six stripes on the U.S. food pyramid.

The stripes stand for the five different food groups plus oils.

GRAINS
VEGETABLES
FRUITS
OILS
MILK
MEAT
& BEANS

This book is about the meat and beans group.

# MEATS!

Meats belong on the purple stripe in the U.S. food pyramid. Meats give us protein. Protein helps our bodies grow. Beans, eggs, and seeds also give us protein.

There are many different foods in this group.

**MEAT**  steak  hamburger

**POULTRY**  chicken  turkey

**FISH** 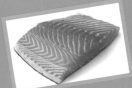 salmon  tuna

**NUTS** almonds   peanut butter

**SEEDS**  sunflower seeds  pumpkin seeds

**EGGS** white chicken eggs  brown chicken eggs

You need food from this group every day.

# BEANS AND PEAS!

Beans and peas belong on two stripes in the U.S. food pyramid. They belong on the purple stripe, with meats, and the green stripe, with vegetables.

There are many kinds of beans and peas.

Beans and peas can be used to make many delicious dishes.

black bean soup

baked beans

hummus

tofu

refried beans

Try to eat some beans or peas every day.

# AROUND THE WORLD

**NORTH AMERICA**

quail

alligator

iguana

**SOUTH AMERICA**

People eat many kinds of meat, poultry, and fish.

octopus

snake meat

sashimi
(raw fish)

EUROPE

ASIA

AFRICA

crocodile

snail

grasshoppers

AUSTRALIA

# How Much Do You Need?

You need to eat three to four ounces (85–113 grams) from the meat and beans group every day.

Three ounces of meat is about the size of a deck of cards.

# HERE IS WHAT COUNTS AS ABOUT THREE OUNCES:

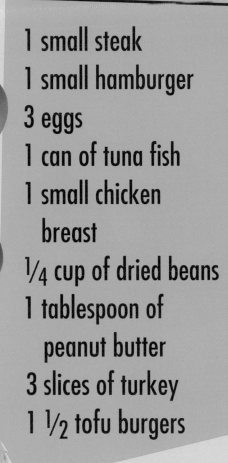

| | |
|---|---|
| 1 small steak | 36 almonds |
| 1 small hamburger | 20 cashew nuts |
| 3 eggs | 21 walnut halves |
| 1 can of tuna fish | 9 thin slices of ham |
| 1 small chicken breast | 1 1/2 cups of split pea soup |
| 1/4 cup of dried beans | 1 1/2 cups of lentil soup |
| 1 tablespoon of peanut butter | 10 medium cooked shrimp |
| 3 slices of turkey | |
| 1 1/2 tofu burgers | |

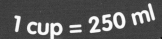

1 cup = 250 ml          1/2 cup = 125 ml

# KEEPING YOU HEALTHY

Meats and beans help keep you healthy.

Meats and beans help build strong bones.

Meats and beans help give your muscles energy.

Meats and beans help you make red bloodcells.

Meats and beans help your body heal cuts and bruises.

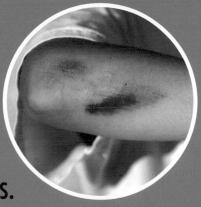

Meats and beans help you fight germs.

Meats and beans have a lot of vitamins and minerals.

15

# Vegetarians

People who do not eat meat are called vegetarians. Vegetarians can stay healthy by eating a lot of beans, seeds, and nuts.

Vegetarians enjoy meals without meat.

veggie pizza

bean burritos

tofu-vegetable
stir-fry

vegetable
lasagna

lentil burgers

vegetable
kabobs

Some vegetarians also drink milk and eat eggs.

# ANY TIME

Almost any time is a good time to eat foods from the meat and beans group.

You can have eggs for breakfast.

You can have
a chicken sandwich
for lunch.

You can snack on some
peanut butter after school.

You can have
a shrimp taco
for dinner.

Try to eat only lean meats and skinless chicken.

# AMAZING FACTS

The ancient Romans believed chicken bones held the power to tell the future.

In 1621, the first Thanksgiving feast probably did not include turkey. It did include goose, codfish, and lobster.

The word "frankfurter" comes from Frankfurt, Germany. The German sausage served here was made of pork.

Benjamin Franklin was a vegetarian.

In 1992, people made an egg omelet that weighed 6,510 pounds (2,953 kilograms). That is about 3 tons!

China now raises more chickens than any other country in the world.

An average hen lays 300 to 325 eggs a year. She starts laying eggs at 19 weeks of age.

As a hen grows older, she produces larger eggs.

Chicken eggs weigh about 100 times more than hummingbird eggs.

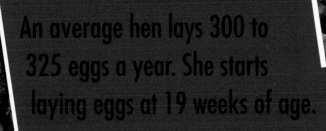

Ostrich eggs weigh about 25 times more than chicken eggs.

# WORLD FOOD GUIDES

The U.S. food pyramid is only one guide to eating well.

To learn more about Canada's Food Guide, check out the Web site below.

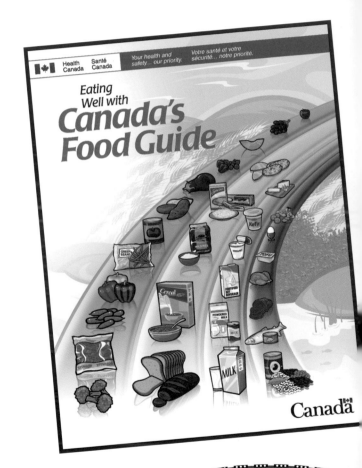

www.nms.on.ca/Elementary/canada.htm

People from different parts of the world often eat different kinds of foods. People use different food guides to help them eat wisely.

The Vegan Food Pyramid

Vegetable Oils and Fats
Some sweets, salt, spices, Nuts,

Use Sparingly

Fortified Dairy Substitutes
2-3 Servings

Eat Moderately

Legumes, Seeds
Beans Group
2-3 Servings

Eat Moderately

VeganFoodPyramid.com

Whole Grains, Bread
Rice and Pasta, Cereal Group
6-11 Servings

Eat Generously

The Veggie Group
3-5 Servings

Eat Liberally

The Fruit Group
2-4 Servings

Eat Liberally

Water
8-10 Glasses a day. If you are active, drink more!

Vegans do not get protein from meat or milk.

# WORDS TO KNOW

 hummus

 iguana

 quail

 refried beans

 sashimi (raw fish)

 tofu

# FIND OUT MORE

## Books

*Meat And Beans,* Emily K. Green, Children's Press.

*Hubert the Pudge: A Vegetarian Tale,* Henrik Drescher, Candlewick.

## Web Sites

MyPyramid.gov
*www.mypyramid.gov/kids/index.html*

Slim Goodbody
*www.slimgoodbody.com*

Printed in the U.S.A.-CG